Pilot Mom

Kathleen Benner Duble

Illustrated by Alan Marks

TALEWINDS

A Charlesbridge Imprint

"Time to suit up!" my best friend, K. C., shouts.

I open one eye and squint sleepily up at her. Today my mom is taking K. C. and me to the air base, so I can show my best friend what my mom does. My mom is a tanker pilot.

After we tour the base, my mom is going away. She's leaving this afternoon to go to Europe on a training mission. For two weeks, it'll be just my dad and me. My dad's a salesman. He's coming back today from his own trip and will meet us at the air base.

Three years ago my mom went to Saudi Arabia to fly in the Gulf War. She was gone four months. I would sometimes see the news on TV about the war. I would see bombs going off and buildings on fire. I don't want my mom to go again.

K. C. rips off my covers. "Rise and shine, soldier," she calls out.

I sit up slowly. My mom is in the room, too. She has on her flight suit. It's green and all one piece.

She walks over and touches my face. Her fingers are warm on my cheek. I think about her leaving, and my stomach does a flip-flop.

"Take your time," she whispers in my ear. She knows I'm slow to wake up.

K. C. puts on a jumpsuit. It's all one piece, too, but it's lime green. I laugh. I think it's funny that she wants to look like my mom.

"I wish I had a suit the same color as yours," K. C. says to my mom.

My mom smiles. "Only the government can produce this color, K. C."

I swing my legs off the bed and go to help my mom fill the pockets of her flight suit. We do this every time she goes to work. It's our special routine. But today is different. Today she is going far away. I picture her flying over the ocean, where if something should happen, she would be alone in cold, deep water. I am slower than usual this morning.

I put my mom's line badge in her top left pocket. It's her identification. I like the picture of my mom on the badge. She looks beautiful in it.

My mom goes to tie her survival pocketknife to her uniform by her left thigh.

"What's that for?" K. C. asks my mom.

My mom opens the small switchblade on the knife. "The blade is for survival purposes, to get food if you need it."

Then she opens the hook blade. "If I have to bail out, this is to cut my parachute lines should they get tangled up."

"You could use the pocketknife if you were in the middle of nowhere all alone, right?" I say.

"Yes," says my mom.

I think of my mom all by herself somewhere. I think of the ocean again.

"You can open a can of beans with it," I tell K. C.

"Only if you take a can with you when you jump out of the plane," says my mom. Then she laughs and winks at me.

K. C. and I laugh, too. It is a silly idea.

"Okay, Jenny," my mom says. "Where are my flight gloves?"

I get her gloves and hat and put them in her right leg pocket. I add a pen and pencil to the left sleeve pocket. Then I stick my mom's name tag onto the Velcro of her uniform. The name tag says Major Strom.

"We have to wear name tags on field trips from school," K. C. says. "Is that so you won't get lost, too?"

My mom smiles at me. "Do *I* ever get lost, Jenny?" she asks.

It's never my mom who gets lost. It's always my dad. He never asks for directions. If he were a pilot and were lost, he would be lost for a long time.

"Never," I say confidently. I hand her a 1921 silver dollar.

"What's that for?" K. C. asks.

"For luck," I say. "It was my great-grandfather's lucky coin. He gave it to my grandmother when she had my father. And my dad gave it to my mom on the day I was born."

"Jenny was my first and only," my mom says, hugging me tight. "And I carry the silver dollar, and the luck it gives *me*, right near my heart."

She slips the silver dollar into her top left pocket, and I make a wish that she won't really need the luck.

"What's it like when you're flying up there?" K. C. asks.

My mom smiles. "It's beautiful. Sometimes the moon is rising on one side and the sun is going down on the other, just light and sky—and me a part of it all. There's nothing like it."

I wonder if she thinks of me when she's up there flying in all that light and space.

After I dress, we drive to the air base. At the entrance is a guard station. My mom has to show her ID. The guard salutes my mom. My mom salutes the guard. K. C. gives a salute, too. But I wish that we were saluting the guard after my mother had come home safely.

When we walk into the squadron, K. C. looks at the concrete walls and beat-up old desks. She seems disappointed.

"It's not very pretty," I say, wishing she were impressed.

My mom's boss comes by to say hello. He's a colonel and has an eagle patch on each shoulder of his uniform. "Hello, Jenny," the colonel says. "What are you doing here today?"

"I'm showing my best friend, K. C., what my mom does before she leaves," I say.

"Very good," the colonel says. "I hope your friend will see what an important job your mother does here and how valuable she is to us in an emergency."

"Yes, sir," I say. My mom is always valuable to me in an emergency, like the time I broke my arm.

"What happens if there's an emergency?" K. C. asks.

"When there's an emergency," my mom answers, "we have only a few minutes to get to our planes and take off."

"My mom and the other pilots in her squadron would be some of the first ones out to help defend our country," I say. "That's their assigned mission." I know this is important, yet my heart beats fast when I say it.

My mom goes off to talk to another pilot.

"Has your mom ever had an emergency?" K. C. whispers to me.

I nod. "My mom was flying a small plane in a storm during her pilot training," I whisper back. "The line between her fuel tanks clogged, and she had more gas on one side than on the other."

"What's wrong with that?" K. C. whispers.

"It makes it tough to land," I say. "With too much fuel on one side, the plane is really hard to control and could crash."

K. C. looks at my mom, who is now signing papers. "Wow," says K. C.

I nod again. "She landed safely, though, and everyone clapped and cheered because she stayed so calm and did everything right."

"Come on, Jenny," my mom says. "Let's show K. C. the helmets."

I take K. C. to the flight-gear room. The walls are lined with rows and rows of lockers, all containing helmets and flight equipment.

"Cool," says K. C.

K. C. is right. The helmets do look cool.

My mom lets K. C. and me try on some helmets. I give commands through my mask, like my mom has shown me how to do. "Jenny Strom to tower one. Request emergency permission to land on runway nine." I make booming sounds like thunder.

K. C. imitates me. "K. C. to tower one. Request emergency permission to land on runway nine."

A man with some papers walks by and smiles. "Permission granted," he says to K. C. and me.

K. C. and I turn our arms this way and that as if we are landing our planes.

"Are you both safely down yet?" my mom asks.

"Yes," I say. "We're safely down."

"Let's go see the planes, then," says my mom, taking my hand.

We walk onto the tarmac. The tarmac is the parking place for planes.

"These are the planes I fly," my mom says. "They are called KC-135s."

"Like me!" K. C. beams.

"Look," my mom says. "There's one landing now."

We watch the plane turn in the sky. Its wing catches the sunlight and flashes bright. It's always hard for me to believe that my mom can fly something that big. I squeeze my mom's hand, and she squeezes back. I feel proud of her.

"That's a huge plane," K. C. says.

"Come on," my mom says. "Let's go inside one."

We climb the ladder into one of the planes. K. C. follows quietly behind me.

"These planes fuel other planes high in the air," my mom says.

"Like a gas station," I say to K. C.

"Sort of," my mom says, laughing and ruffling my hair. "As a pilot, I must get this plane in front of another plane. Then someone called a boom operator flies the boom out to the other plane. Once they are hooked up, we begin pumping fuel through the boom. Go on, girls. Climb on down and see."

K. C. and I climb down to the boom operator's spot. We look through the tiny window where the boom operator can see the other plane.

"All this fuel allows the fighter jets to go back into action," I say to K. C.

"You mean if there's a war?" K. C. asks, her eyes wide.

I nod but try not to think about this much.

"Come up front and see the pilot's seat," my mom yells to us.

We walk to the front of the plane. There are four seats. K. C. sits in the pilot's seat, my mom's seat. My mom sits next to her. I stand behind my mom.

"On every flight," my mom says, "there's a pilot, a copilot, a navigator, and a boom operator. Having two pilots ensures the mission's safety in the event that something should happen to one of the pilots."

"Not that things often happen to pilots, right?" I quickly say.

My mom reaches around her seat and pulls me to her. "Not to this pilot," she says.

K. C. pushes the pedals back and forth. She turns the steering wheel from side to side.

"Once, though," my mom continues, "when I was flying in Saudi Arabia, we had to land. I radioed to the tower for the coordinates, but the tower wouldn't answer."

"Why?" K. C. asks, biting a nail.

My mom shrugs. "At first I didn't know. I kept circling and calling in, but they still wouldn't answer. Then I remembered that in Saudi Arabia, they don't think women should be pilots."

"That's terrible," cries K. C.

My mom nods. "It is, isn't it?"

"So what did you do?" K. C. asks.

"I had the copilot, who was a man, make the radio call," my mom says.

"That was smart," I say, impressed.

"Do you think?" my mom says, smiling at me.

We walk to the middle of the plane where there are benches for troops.
K. C. leans out the large door in the middle of the plane. "Do the troops
parachute out?" she asks.

"Not out of this plane," my mom says, "but there are others where they do."

K. C. leans way out.

"Jump," someone yells, and K. C. disappears.

I run to the door and look out. A man in a business suit has caught K. C.
It's my dad.

"Nice catch," my mom says.

My dad smiles up at her. "Jump," he yells up to me after he puts K. C.
down, but I shake my head no. I want to stay with my mom.

Together, she and I go back down the ladder. When we get down, my mom puts her arm around me and pulls me aside. "I *will* be home soon, Jenny," she says.

I nod. Being here, I know she has to go. They need smart, calm pilots like my mom. Still. . . .

My mom knows what I am thinking. "Don't worry," she says. "It's a routine mission. There's *no* war this time. I can call often."

Then she kisses my forehead, and I feel warm inside.

"But what if there *is* a war?" I can't help but ask.

My mom kneels down next to me. "Then there's a war, Jenny," she says. "But someone has to defend our country. This is what I do. I love being your mom, but I love doing this, too. And I do it for you, for your freedom, so you have the freedom to do what you want with your life."

My mom looks out at the planes. "And even if I have to go, I feel all right knowing you and your father have each other," she says.

"You worry about me when you're gone?" I ask. "You think about me when you fly?"

My mom smooths back my hair. "Of course I do, Jenny. I always think about you. I worry if you're happy, if you're eating right, if you're sick, so many things. But knowing that you and your father are together, I worry less. I can fly well and do my job better knowing that you are home and safe and well cared for."

I throw my arms around my mother. I smell the sweet scent of her. "Besides," I whisper into her shoulder, "you are a smart, brave, calm pilot. No one is going to take you down."

My mom laughs and pulls the silver dollar from her pocket. "Not as long as I have this with me here and . . ."

She touches my chest and then hers. ". . . you and your father in my heart."

We walk around the plane toward K. C. and my dad.

I look at my mom, my smart, brave, calm mom, who is also a pilot. "Mom," I say, "I don't think I want to be a pilot when I grow up, but I know I'd like to be a mom."

My mom smiles and pulls me close. "That's the finest job I know, Jenny," she says.

For Tobey and Liza—who've given me
the finest job I know! I love you both!
And with many, many thanks and love
to Lt. Colonel Lauren B. Romain,
pilot and mom—K. B. D.

To Charlotte and Lilly—A. M.

Text copyright © 2003 by Kathleen Benner Duble
Illustrations copyright © 2003 by Alan Marks
All rights reserved, including the right of reproduction in whole or
in part in any form. Charlesbridge, Talewinds, and colophon are
registered trademarks of Charlesbridge Publishing, Inc.

Published by Charlesbridge
85 Main Street
Watertown, MA 02472
(617) 926-0329
www.charlesbridge.com

Illustrations done in watercolors and ink
Display type and text type set in Sabon
Color separations, printing, and binding by P. Chan & Edward, Inc.
Production supervision by Brian G. Walker
Designed by Susan Mallory Sherman

Library of Congress Cataloging-in-Publication Data
Duble, Kathleen Benner.
 Pilot mom / Kathleen Benner Duble ; illustrated by Alan Marks.
  p. cm.
Summary: Jenny and her best friend K.C. accompany Jenny's
mother, a tanker pilot in the Air Force, to the air base, where they
explore her plane, a KC-135, prior to her departure on a training
mission to Europe.
ISBN 1-57091-555-5
 [1. Women air pilots—Fiction. 2. Air pilots, Military—Fiction. 3.
Mothers and daughters—Fiction.] I. Marks, Alan, ill. II. Title.
PZ7.D84955 Pi 2003
 [Fic]—dc21   2002010535

Printed in China
(hc) 10 9 8 7 6 5 4 3 2 1